UNCLE LESTER'S HAT

written and illustrated by

Howie Schneider

G. P. Putnam's Sons • New York

Dedicated to the memory of
Frank Catalano

Library of Congress Cataloging in Publication Data
Schneider, Howie, 1930–
Uncle Lester's hat / by Howie Schneider.   p.   cm.
Summary: Lazy Uncle Wilfred finds adventure beyond his television
set when he tries to retrieve his uncle's flyaway hat.
[1. Hats—Fiction.   2. Uncles—Fiction.]   I. Title.
PZ7.S3633Un   1993   [E]—dc20   92-20750   CIP   AC
ISBN 0-399-22439-4

1   3   5   7   9   10   8   6   4   2

First Impression

My uncle Wilfred never went out much. He just sat in his favorite chair all day and watched TV. "It's my back," he said. "It hurts when I walk."

One morning I found him wearing a funny hat. "It belonged to your great uncle Lester, the adventurer," he told me. "Your mother found it in the attic, but it's very dusty. It needs some air."

So Uncle Wilfred went out. "His hat needs some air,"
I told my mother.
"So does Uncle Wilfred," she said.

I watched them cross the street and head for the park.
It looked like there was plenty of air out there.

After that I couldn't see him anymore. I knew he wouldn't be gone long. His back would start to hurt him soon.

My mother told me Uncle Wilfred hated to travel.
"He never goes anywhere," she said.

"'Traveling is a waste of time,' he would say."

" 'If you've seen one place you've seen them all,
just sitting in your nice comfortable chair at home,
watching television,' he said."

I wish he was sitting in it now. He's been gone
a long time.

"Don't worry about Uncle Wilfred," my mother said.

"He's no adventurer like his Uncle Lester was."

"Wilfred likes his comfort too much."

I wish I had known Great Uncle Lester.

He must have been all over the world.

I bet he saw everything there was to see.

Uncle Wilfred just watches TV.

He should have been back by now.

He's missing all his favorite shows.

"I can go clear around the world in the time it takes
to turn on my TV," Uncle Wilfred used to tell me.

"Even your great uncle Lester couldn't do that."

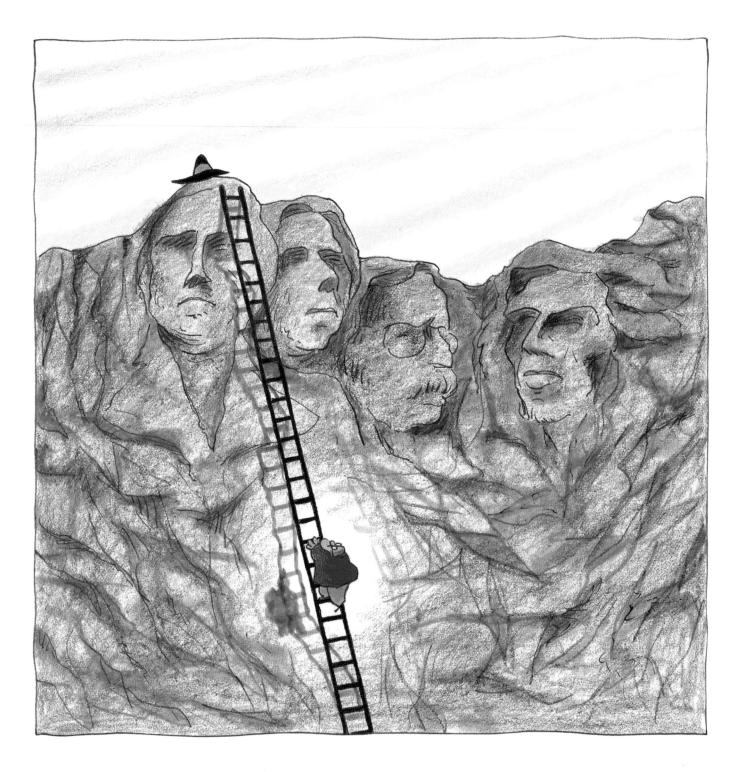

I told him that they didn't have television back in
Great Uncle Lester's time.

"And it must have been a pretty dull life without it,"
he said.

It was a pretty dull life with it too, I thought, if you have to watch all by yourself.

I miss Uncle Wilfred.

Then I saw him. They were back…the hat first,
then Uncle Wilfred.

He looked different. He said his back didn't bother him anymore.

He told me lots of great stories about where he had
been and what he had seen. I could listen to him
for hours.

Uncle Wilfred goes out a lot now. He says that when
I get bigger he's going to give Great Uncle Lester's hat
to me.

I can't wait.

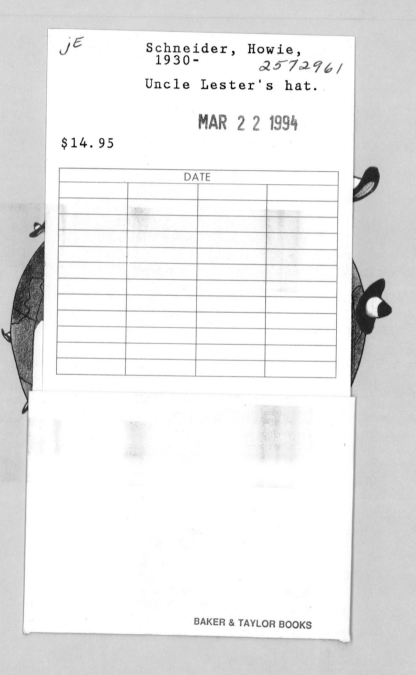